BEN M. BAGLIO

The Midnight Mouse

Illustrated by
Andy Ellis

D1301751

A
LITTLE APPLE
PAPERBACK

SCHOLASTIC INC.

New York Toronto London Auckland Sydney
Mexico City New Delhi Hong Kong Buenos Aires

ISBN 0-439-41916-6

Text copyright © 2001 by Working Partners Limited.
Original series created by Ben M. Baglio.
Illustrations copyright © 2001 by Andy Ellis.

12 11 10 9 8 7 6 5   4 5 6 7 8/0

Printed in the U.S.A.   40
First Scholastic printing, February 2003

To Yvonne, who once saved a mouse
with an oven glove

Special thanks to Narinder Dhami

1

"We're not late, are we, Dad?" Mandy Hope asked. "Amy will be waiting for me."

It was Saturday morning and Dr. Adam Hope was taking Mandy to her friend Amy Fenton's house.

Dr. Adam smiled as he drove past Welford's village green. "Don't worry, dear," he said. "The pet shop won't run out of mice before you and Amy get there!"

"I know, Dad," Mandy said with a grin. "But we want to get there early. Amy says it's going to take ages to find just the right mouse!"

Mandy loved animals. Her mom and dad were both vets.

There were always animals around at Animal Ark, their clinic. Today, Amy was going to buy a pet mouse. She'd asked Mandy to come and help her choose.

"Make sure you and Amy look for a healthy mouse, won't you, Mandy?" said Dr. Adam as they pulled up outside Amy's house.

"Yes, Dad," she said. "What should we look out for?"

"Well, a healthy mouse will have nice bright eyes and clean fur," said Dr. Adam. "Has Amy bought a cage for the mouse yet?"

Mandy shook her head. "No, she's buying *everything* today."

"Hamster cages are good for mice, too," Dr. Adam said as Mandy undid her seatbelt. "They're large and roomy, and they have a wheel for exercise. But make sure the mouse can't squeeze through the bars of the cage and escape. Mice are a little thinner than hamsters!"

Mandy laughed. "I'll remember that, Dad!" she said.

Just then the Fentons' front door opened, and Amy came rushing out. "Mandy!" she shouted, "I thought you were *never* coming! Hello, Dr. Adam."

Dr. Adam waved at her. "Good luck with the mouse hunt

today, Amy!" he said with a grin.
Then he drove off.

Amy grabbed Mandy's hand.
"I'm so excited!" she said happily.
"I can't *wait* to get my very own
pet!"

Mandy grinned back. She
couldn't wait, either! Life at
Animal Ark was too busy for

Mandy to have a pet of her own.
But it was great fun to share her
friends' pets.

"Hello, Mandy," Amy's mom
said, following Amy out of the
house. "Let's go right away, girls.
The pet shop will be very busy
later on. It always is on
Saturdays."

The pet shop was in Walton,
the nearby town. As they drove
along, Amy was so excited she
couldn't sit still. Mandy just hoped
that there were lots of mice to
choose from.

And there *were* lots to choose
from! Mandy could hardly believe
her eyes. She stood in the pet shop

and stared at all the glass tanks
full of mice.

There were white ones, black
ones, gray ones, and cream-and-
brown ones, all snuggled up
together.

"Wow!" Amy said happily.
"Just look at all these lovely mice!"

The pet shop wasn't very busy
yet because it was still early. So

Mandy, Amy, and Mrs. Fenton could take their time.

"Do you know what color mouse you would like?" asked Mr. Piper, the pet-shop owner.

Mandy liked Mr. Piper. Her friend Peter Foster bought dog chews from him for his pup, Timmy.

Amy thought for a bit. She walked up and down, looking into the glass tanks.

Mandy looked, too. She really liked the fluffy cream-colored ones. But then she liked the sweet little gray ones with pink noses, too. *And* the snowy white ones! She knew that *she* would find it *very* hard to choose!

At last Amy stopped at the tank with white mice. "I'd like a white one, please," she said.

Mr. Piper smiled and nodded. He carefully lifted the lid from the tank. "Is there one special mouse you'd like to look at, my dear?" he asked.

Mandy and Amy looked into the tank, their noses pressed up against the glass.

"I just don't know!" Amy said. "They're *all* cute."

But Mandy was watching one little mouse in the corner. She scratched around, waving her long pink tail. Then she ran over and jumped playfully onto another mouse who was having a snooze. Mandy grinned and gave Amy a nudge.

The mouse saw Amy and

Mandy looking at her through the glass. She padded over on her tiny pink paws, sat up on her back legs, and stared right back at them, pink nose twitching.

Mandy looked at her shiny black eyes and smooth snowy coat. "She looks healthy," she said happily.

"And she's got the sweetest pink ears. And look at her long whiskers!" said Amy. She looked at her mom. "Do you like her, too, Mom?"

Mrs. Fenton smiled. "Yes, dear," she said. "She seems very lively."

Amy turned to Mr. Piper, then pointed to the mouse. "That's the one I want, please!"

2

"Come on, Mousey!" Amy said proudly as she carried her new pet into the Fentons' house. "This is your new home!"

Mandy laughed as she followed Amy inside. "You'll have to think of a good name for her."

Amy nodded. She put the cage down on the living room floor. The mouse was running around her new home, checking it out.

Mandy had told Amy what her dad had said, and Amy had chosen a cage with narrow spaces between the bars. It also had a wheel and a little hut for sleeping in. They'd bought some bedding, some bags of food, and a water bottle from the pet shop, too.

"Hello, Mousey," Mandy said. She bent down to look in the cage. The mouse was busy making herself a cozy bed.

"Can you think of a good name for her, Mandy?" Amy asked.

"What about Snowy?" Mandy said.

Amy shook her head. "How about Fluffy?"

Mandy thought. "She doesn't *look* like a Fluffy," she said.

Amy looked at her mouse. "You're right," she said. She sighed.

"Never mind. We'll think of something!" said Mandy. "Are you going to take her out of the cage?"

Amy looked a little worried. "I'm not sure how to hold her," she said.

"I've seen Mom and Dad pick

up mice at Animal Ark," Mandy told her. "Should I show you?"

Amy nodded.

"I'd better shut the door first," said Mrs. Fenton, coming into the living room. "I don't want Ms. Mouse running all over the house!" she joked.

Carefully, Mandy opened the cage. She took hold of the mouse's tail with one hand and slid her other hand under its furry little body.

"Doesn't it hurt her when you hold her by the tail like that?" Amy asked, chewing a fingernail.

Mandy shook her head. "No,

not if you put your other hand underneath her. But my mom told me that you should *never* pick up a mouse just by its tail."

The mouse didn't seem to mind being picked up at all. She sat happily on Mandy's hand, cleaning her whiskers and looking at the girls with her bright eyes.

Mandy carefully passed her to Amy. The mouse sniffed at Amy's hand and then tried to disappear up the sleeve of her sweater, squeaking as she went. Mandy and Amy burst out laughing.

"I think she likes you, Amy!" Mandy said.

Just then, the phone rang. Mrs. Fenton picked it up. Mandy and Amy were too busy playing with the mouse to listen to what Amy's mom was saying.

Mrs. Fenton put down the phone. "Your uncle Jack's got the flu," she told Amy. "He and your aunt Jenny were going to London today. They've got tickets for a show tonight and they've booked a hotel room. But now they can't go. So they've asked if your dad and I would like to go instead."

"That sounds great!" Amy said. "Are you going to say yes?"

Her mom shook her head. "I

said we couldn't. There isn't time to find someone to come and look after you, dear." She smiled and gave Amy a hug. "Never mind," she said. "We can *all* go another time." But Mandy suddenly had a

really good idea. She jumped to her feet. "Amy and her mouse could come and stay at Animal Ark tonight!" she said.

"Oh, yes, please!" said Amy. "We'd love that, wouldn't we, Mousey?"

"Well, that's very nice of you, Mandy," said Mrs. Fenton with a smile. "But don't you think you'd better phone and ask your mom first?"

Mandy nodded, but she was sure her mom would say yes. She picked up the Fentons' phone and dialed Animal Ark.

Emily Hope answered the phone, and Mandy told her mom

what had happened. "So can Amy and her mouse come and stay with us tonight, Mom?" she finished.

"Of course, they can," Dr. Emily said. "I'm looking forward to meeting Amy's new pet."

"Oh, great!" said Mandy. "Thanks, Mom!"

3

"So this is the famous mouse!" Dr. Adam said as Amy and Mandy brought the cage into Animal Ark's kitchen. Mr. and Mrs. Fenton had dropped the girls off on their way to London.

"Very sweet!" said Dr. Emily. "Have you come up with a name?"

Amy and Mandy looked at each other. "Not yet," they said together.

"What about Maxwell?" Dr. Adam suggested as he made some coffee.

Mandy and Amy burst out laughing.

"Yes, that's a great name, Dad!" Mandy said. "But it's a boy's name. This mouse is a girl!"

Dr. Adam raised his eyebrows, then bent down and stared at the mouse.

The mouse stared back. She twitched her nose at him, then ran into her hut.

Dr. Adam grinned. "Oh, yes, so she is," he said. He went back to making his coffee.

Mandy and Amy carried the mouse's cage upstairs to Mandy's bedroom. They put it on Mandy's desk, and a few seconds later the mouse popped out of her hut. She had a good look around and then sat down to wash herself.

"She knows she's somewhere different!" Amy said.

"I just wish we could think of a name for her," Mandy said as the mouse began to clean her pink ears with her tiny paws.

"Mandy," said Amy.

"What?" asked Mandy.

"No, I mean what about *Mandy*?" Amy said. "Mandy Mouse!"

The two girls laughed.

"Mandy Hope sounds all right, but Mandy Mouse is a little funny!" said Mandy.

"Look, I think she wants to go to sleep," Amy said. The mouse had gone back into her hut and was curling up in the soft bedding.

"Let's let her take her nap,"

said Mandy. So they tiptoed out
of the bedroom and went
downstairs.

Dr. Adam and Dr. Emily were
in the Animal Ark office doing
some paperwork.

"I've got a great name for

your mouse, Amy!" Mandy's dad called. "How about Minnie?"

Amy frowned. "I like that name, Dr. Adam," she said. "But this mouse doesn't *look* like a Minnie."

"Well, what about Mavis?" asked Dr. Adam.

"Mavis?" said Mandy and Amy together, shaking their heads.

"Molly?" asked Dr. Emily.

But Amy shook her head again. "She's not a Mavis or a Molly," she said.

"What about Polly?" Mandy asked. "Or Sugar? Barbie? Susie?"

But Amy didn't think any of them were right for her mouse.

"We'll just have to think a little more!" she said.

Mandy and Amy decided to find some toys for the mouse to play with when she woke up. But they didn't know what she would like, so they asked Dr. Emily.

"Well, mice are the same as hamsters," Mandy's mom said. "They like tunnels and things they can run and jump into. So the tubes from toilet paper and kitchen paper towel rolls are good. So are small cardboard boxes. They can hide in them, and then chew them to pieces!"

"Let's look around the house and see what we can find," Mandy said to Amy.

They found a toilet paper roll in the bathroom wastebasket, and Mandy's dad gave them some small cardboard boxes from the clinic. Then Mandy found a little ladder in her toy box, which had come from her old dollhouse.

Dr. Adam cooked dinner while Dr. Emily did evening rounds at Animal Ark.

After they'd eaten, Mandy and Amy went back upstairs to see if the mouse was awake yet. They found her sitting up on her hind legs, nibbling seeds from her food dish.

"She's having her dinner, too!" said Amy.

When she'd finished eating, Mandy and Amy had great fun showing the mouse all her new toys.

The mouse seemed to like them all. First, she climbed up and down the ladder.

Then she dashed back and
forth through the cardboard tunnel.

She jumped in and out of the
boxes. Then she sat down to chew
them to pieces!

Mandy and Amy played with the mouse until Dr. Emily came in and said it was time for bed. She brought in a cot for Amy and put it next to Mandy's bed.

"Now make sure you go to sleep," Dr. Emily said as she turned out the light. "No sneaking out of bed to play with the mouse!"

"Good night, Mandy," whispered Amy. "Thanks for helping me with my mouse."

"It was fun!" Mandy said. She yawned. "Good night, Amy. Good night, Mousey!" Maybe tomorrow she and Amy would be able to think of a really good name for the mouse. . . .

Squ-e-e-e-ak!

Slowly, Mandy opened her eyes. Was she dreaming? She'd just heard a very funny sound.

Squ-e-e-e-ak!

No, she *wasn't* dreaming. There it was again! Mandy looked at her bedside clock. The glowing numbers told her it was very, very late — midnight!

Squ-e-e-e-ak!

4

Mandy sat up in bed.

So did Amy. "What's that noise, Mandy?" she asked. "Is it my mouse?"

Mandy shook her head. "I don't know," she said. "I've never heard it before."

Squ-e-e-e-e-ak! The noise came again.

"Mandy, Animal Ark doesn't

have a ghost, does it?" Amy asked. She sounded really scared.

"No, of *course* not!" Mandy said. But now she felt a tiny bit scared herself.

Squ-e-e-e-ak! Squ-e-e-e-ak! SQU-E-E-E-AK! The noise was getting louder and louder.

"What is it, then?" asked Amy, putting her hands over her ears. Then she gasped, her eyes wide. "Oh! It isn't my mouse, is it?"

Mandy shook her head. "No, it doesn't sound like a mouse at all!" she said.

They both listened hard.

Mandy switched on her bedside light and pushed back the

blanket. "I think it's coming from over by the mouse's cage, though."

Her mom had told them not to get out of bed, but she just *had* to find out what the squeaking was!

"Is she all right?" Amy asked, looking worried. She got out of bed, too, and followed Mandy across the room.

Mandy looked into the cage.
Then she began to laugh. The
mouse was running around on
her wheel. And every time the
wheel went around, it squeaked.
The faster the mouse ran, the
louder the wheel squeaked!

Amy looked over Mandy's shoulder. "Oh, it's the wheel!" she said, and she began to laugh, too.

Mandy opened the cage door and gently lifted the mouse off her wheel. But as soon as Mandy put her down, the mouse jumped back on and started running again. *Squ-e-e-e-ak!*

"Let's give her some food," Mandy said. "Maybe that will stop her."

But the mouse didn't want any food. All she wanted to do was play on her wheel. She was enjoying her new game!

"Let's take the wheel out of the cage," Amy said.

But the wheel was fixed very firmly. Mandy was worried they might break it if they pulled it hard.

"What are we going to do?" Amy asked, putting her hands over her ears again. "We'll *never* get back to sleep with all this squeaking!"

5

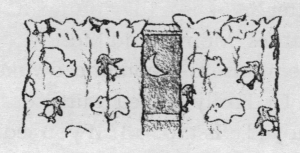

"I'll have to go and tell Mom and Dad," said Mandy.

Amy looked worried. "Will they be very mad?"

"I hope not!" Mandy said.

She crept into her mom and dad's bedroom and gave her dad's shoulder a little shake.

"Wh-a-a-h!" her dad said, waking up with a jolt.

That woke up Dr. Emily, too.

"Mandy!" she said. "What are you doing up? Is something the matter?"

"Yes, Mom," said Mandy. "The mouse is keeping us awake!"

Dr. Emily looked a little annoyed. "Is that all? If you leave her alone she'll settle down."

"Yes," Dr. Adam agreed. "Now back to bed!"

"But, Dad, she won't stop running around on her wheel," Mandy told him. "And the wheel's making a horrible squeaking noise!"

Dr. Adam and Dr. Emily looked at each other.

"It can't be that bad, Mandy," said her mom.

"It is, Mom!" Mandy said. "We have to put our hands over our ears!"

Dr. Adam yawned. "I'll come and have a look," he said, getting out of bed.

Before they even went into Mandy's bedroom, they could hear *squeak, squeak, squ-e-e-ak!*

"Goodness me," said Dr. Adam, looking surprised. "That *is* loud!"

"I told you so, Dad!" said Mandy.

Dr. Adam went to look in the cage. He began to laugh as he saw the mouse running around in the wheel as fast as she could.

"She should be in the Olympics!" he said. "I've never seen such a fast runner!"

"She's been running for ages now," said Amy. "She must be tired."

"She might be feeling a little

upset," Dr. Adam said. "After all, she's been to *two* different places today. When she settles down, she'll stop using the wheel so much."

"But how are we going to get to sleep tonight, Dad?" Mandy asked.

"I've got just the thing!" Dr. Adam said, winking at them.

He went out and came back a few minutes later carrying a can of oil. "This will do the trick!" he said.

Amy took the mouse off the wheel and held her while Dr. Adam put some oil on it. Then she put the mouse back in her cage.

They all watched as she hopped onto the wheel again. This time there was not a squeak to be heard!

"Phew!" said Amy and Mandy together.

"Thanks, Dr. Adam!" Amy added.

Mandy gave her dad a hug.

"I think she'll go to sleep soon, anyway," said Dr. Adam. "Mice

"What's so funny?" Amy asked, sitting up in bed and rubbing her eyes.

"Mousey's on her wheel again!" Mandy said. She grinned at her friend. "We can't keep calling her 'Mousey,' Amy! We'll have to think of a name soon."

Amy smiled. "I've *got* a name for her!" she said.

"Oh!" Mandy was very surprised. "What is it? When did you think of it?" she asked.

"I thought of it just before I went back to sleep last night," Amy said. "I'm going to call her Squeaker!"

Mandy burst out laughing. "That's a great name, Amy!" she said. "It really suits her!"

Amy nodded. "And it'll always remind me of last night!" she said with a grin.

"Come on, let's go and tell Mom and Dad," Mandy said. She and Amy picked up Squeaker's cage and went downstairs.

Dr. Adam and Dr. Emily were

already in the kitchen having breakfast.

"So how's the mouse this morning?" Dr. Adam asked. "She's not being too noisy, I hope?"

"Don't call her 'the mouse,' Dad," Mandy said, grinning. "She *has* a name!"

"She does?" Dr. Adam asked, raising his eyebrows.

"I thought you couldn't decide what to call her," said Dr. Emily.

"I made up my mind last night," Amy said. "I'm going to call her Squeaker!"

Dr. Adam and Dr. Emily smiled.

"That's a very good name, Amy," said Mandy's dad. He looked at Squeaker, who was having a drink of water from her bottle. "But I hope Squeaker never squeaks as loudly as her wheel did!"

In the afternoon, Mr. and Mrs. Fenton came to pick up Amy and Squeaker.

Mandy and Amy were watching for their car. They went to the door to meet them, taking Squeaker with them in her cage.

"Hi, Mom, hi, Dad!" Amy said. "Did you have a good time?"

"Yes, thanks, dear, we did," said her dad, coming in through the door.

Mrs. Fenton followed him in and closed the door behind her. "And how's Ms. Mouse?" she asked.

"*Squeaker*'s fine!" said Amy.

Her mom and dad looked surprised. *"Squeaker?"* they said together.

Amy nodded. "That's what I'm calling her!" she said, taking Squeaker out of her cage to show them.

"That's a good name for a mouse!" Mrs. Fenton said. "But how on earth did you think of it?"

Mandy and Amy looked at each other and burst out laughing.

Dr. Emily came out from the kitchen. "Come in and have a cup of coffee," she said. "And we'll tell you all about it!"